Where Does the Butterfly Go When It Rains?

by MAY GARELICK

Illustrated by
NICHOLAS WILTON

For my daughter Hannah—N.W.

The illustrations are painted on illustration board using acrylic gesso and acrylic paints. The painted surfaces are sanded and scraped with various tools to help create some of the background textures.

For information contact:
MONDO Publishing
980 Avenue of the Americas
New York, New York 10018
Visit our web site at http://www.mondopub.com

Printed in Hong Kong
02 03 04 05   9 8 7 6 5 4 3

Designed by Mina Greenstein
Production by Danny Adlerman

Library of Congress Cataloging-in-Publication Data
Garelick, May, 1910-
Where does the butterfly go when it rains? / by May Garelick ; illustrated by Nicholas Wilton.
p.   cm.
Originally published: New York : W.R. Scott, © 1961.
Summary: Illustrations and simple text describe what different animals do when it rains.
ISBN 1-57255-165-8 (hardcover : alk. paper). — ISBN 1-57255-162-3 (pbk : alk. paper)
[1. Rain and rainfall—Fiction. 2. Animals—Fiction.] I. Wilton, NIcholas, ill. II. Title.
PZ7.G17935Wh   1997
[E]—dc20   96-27575
                                                                CIP
                                                                 AC

Where Does the Butterfly Go When It Rains?

Rain. Rain. Rain. Rain.
Where does the butterfly go
when it rains?

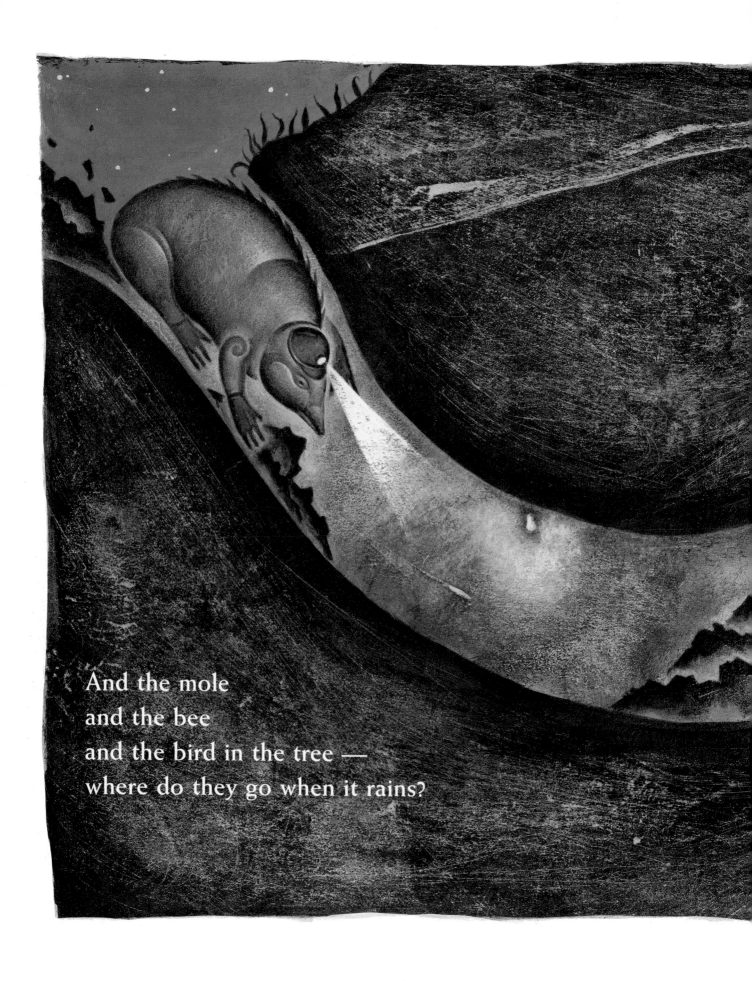

And the mole
and the bee
and the bird in the tree —
where do they go when it rains?

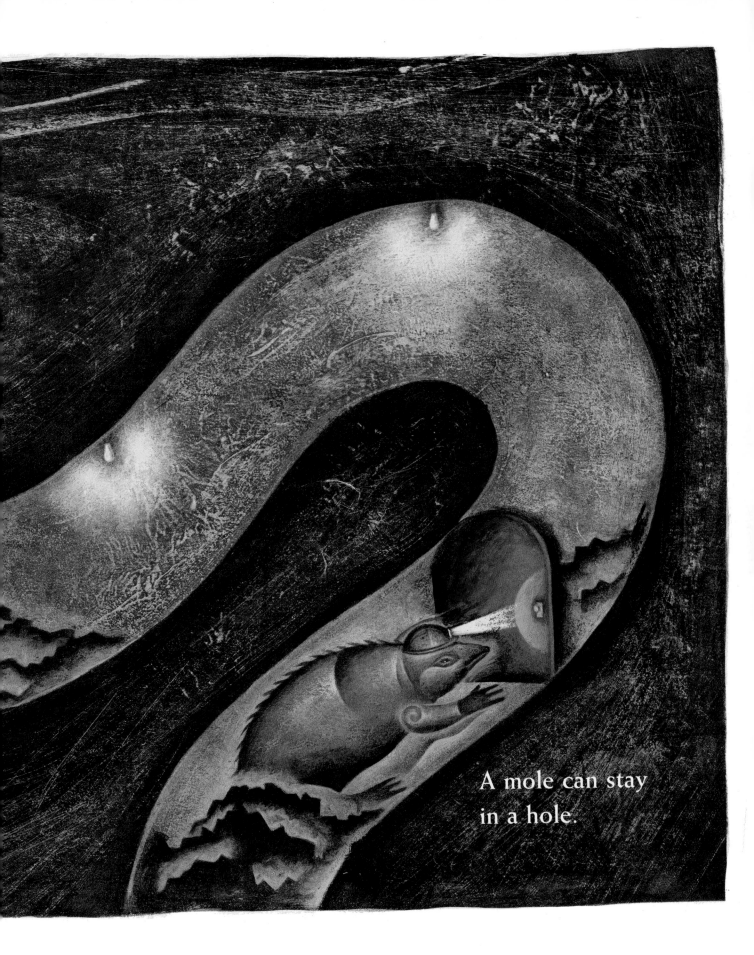

A mole can stay
in a hole.

A bee can fly back to the hive.

I've heard
that a bird
tucks its head under its wing.

But where does the butterfly go
when it rains?

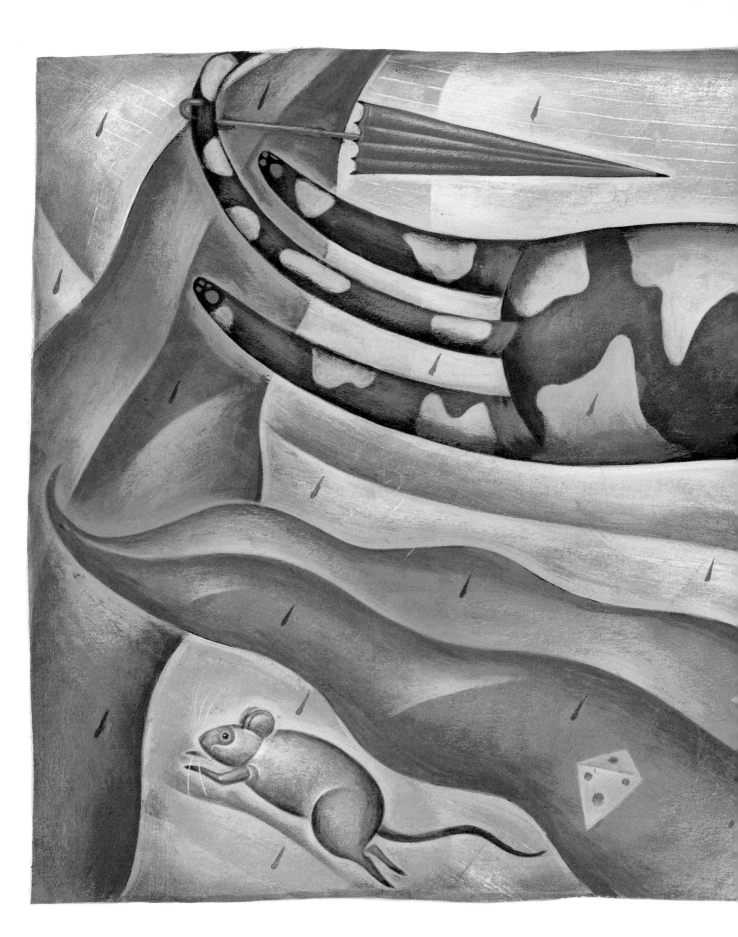

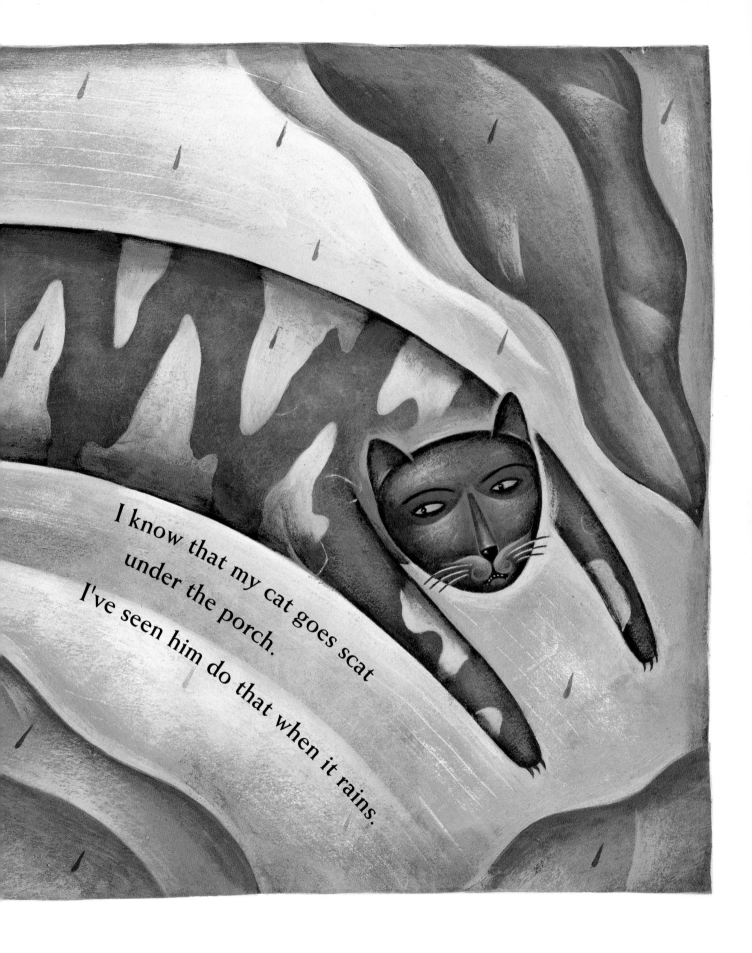

I know that my cat goes scat
under the porch.
I've seen him do that when it rains.

A snake,
I suppose,
can slide between rocks.

A grasshopper can hide
in tall grass.

A rabbit can dash —
whoosh — into a bush.

But where does the butterfly go
when it rains?

The cows I see in the field
just stand in the rain and get wet.
They eat and get wet
and eat and get wetter.
Don't cows mind the rain?

I know why a duck doesn't mind the rain.
Someone told me.

A duck's feathers
are oily and slick,
so the rain doesn't stick.
Water slides off a duck's back.
Quack. Quack.

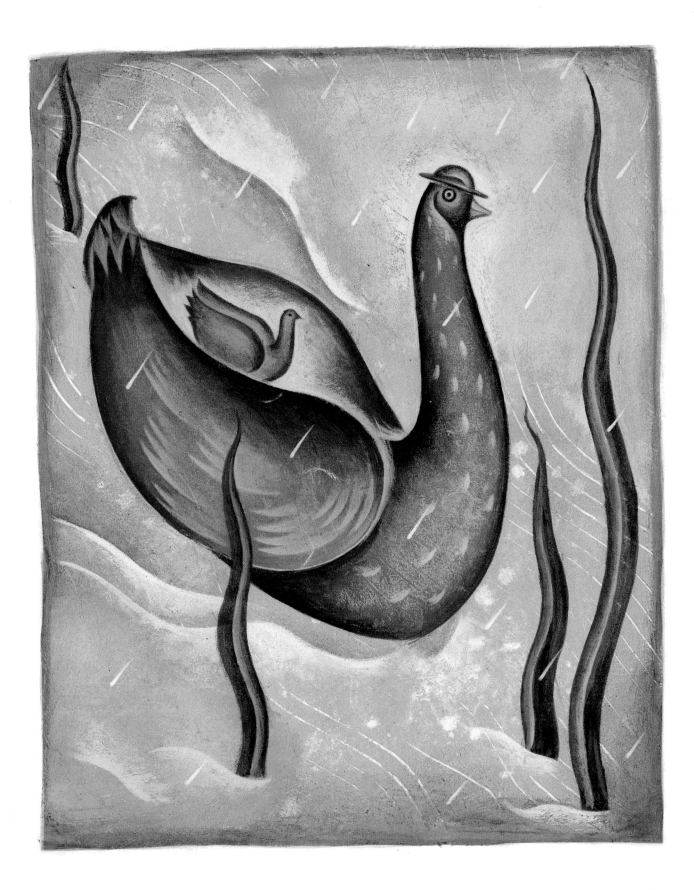

But what about minnows
and how about trout?

Where do fish go when it rains?

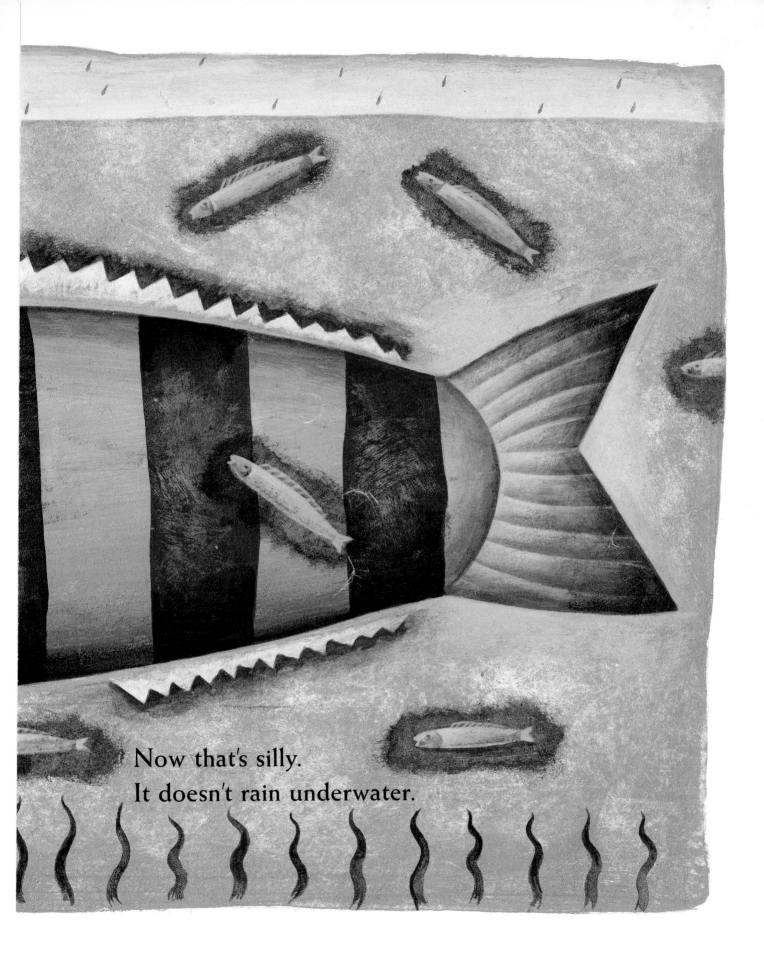

Now that's silly.
It doesn't rain underwater.

But what can a butterfly do?
How can it fly if its wings are wet?
Where does the butterfly go
when it rains?

And the bird in the tree
is a puzzle to me.
Even if its head is tucked
under its wing,
what happens to the rest of it,
poor thing?

As soon as the rain
stops raining so hard,
I'll go quietly
up to a tree.
And maybe I'll find
a bird in that tree,
and I'll see
what it does in the rain.

Maybe I'll find
a butterfly, too.
Then I'll know what it does
when it rains.

But where can I look?
I've never seen a butterfly
out in the rain.
Have you?